Dear Parent:
Your child's love of reading starts here!

Every child learns to read in a different way and at his or her own speed. Some go back and forth between reading levels and read favorite books again and again. Others read through each level in order. You can help your young reader improve and become more confident by encouraging his or her own interests and abilities. From books your child reads with you to the first books he or she reads alone, there are I Can Read Books for every stage of reading:

SHARED READING
Basic language, word repetition, and whimsical illustrations, ideal for sharing with your emergent reader

BEGINNING READING
Short sentences, familiar words, and simple concepts for children eager to read on their own

READING WITH HELP
Engaging stories, longer sentences, and language play for developing readers

READING ALONE
Complex plots, challenging vocabulary, and high-interest topics for the independent reader

I Can Read Books have introduced children to the joy of reading since 1957. Featuring award-winning authors and illustrators and a fabulous cast of beloved characters, I Can Read Books set the standard for beginning readers.

A lifetime of discovery begins with the magical words **"I Can Read!"**

Visit www.icanread.com for information
on enriching your child's reading experience.

In loving memory of D.N.,
my Ojiji
—M.I.

I Can Read® and I Can Read Book® are trademarks of HarperCollins Publishers.

Gigi and Ojiji
Copyright © 2022 by Melissa Iwai
All rights reserved. Printed in the United States of America.
No part of this book may be used or reproduced in any manner whatsoever without written permission except
in the case of brief quotations embodied in critical articles and reviews. For information address HarperCollins
Children's Books, a division of HarperCollins Publishers, 195 Broadway, New York, NY 10007.
www.icanread.com

Library of Congress Control Number: 2021945750
ISBN 978-0-06-320806-3 (trade bdg.) — ISBN 978-0-06-320805-6 (pbk.)

Book design by Chrisila Maida

22 23 24 25 26 LSCC 10 9 8 7 6 5 4 3 2 1 ❖ First Edition

I Can Read!

3 READING ALONE

GIGI AND OJIJI

MELISSA IWAI

HARPER

An Imprint of HarperCollins Publishers

Gigi was making a special present.
"Ojiisan is going to love this,"
Gigi thought.

Ojiisan means grandfather in Japanese.
Gigi's grandfather was coming from Japan
to live with them.
"We're going to have fun
 with Ojiisan, right, Roscoe?"
"We'll play tag. We'll read books.
We'll teach you new tricks!"

"Ready, Gigi?" her mom called.

"Hai!" said Gigi.

Hai means yes in Japanese.

Gigi practiced her Japanese words
on the way to the airport.
She knew how to say "thank you,"
"good morning," "good night,"
"hello," and how to count to ten.

"Ojiisan is going to be so happy to
hear you speak Japanese!" said Dad.

At the airport,

Gigi and her parents waited

for Ojiisan to arrive.

"There he is!" Mom said.

International Arrivals

"Is that man really Ojiisan?"

asked Gigi.

"He doesn't look like

he can play tag," she thought.

This was not going well.

"This is Gigi," Mom said.
Mom pressed on Gigi's back
to remind her to bow.
Gigi tried to say "hello" in Japanese,
but her tongue got all twisted up.

"What?" Ojiisan said.

"She said konnichiwa," Mom explained.

Ojiisan laughed and nodded his head.

"Konnichiwa!" he said.

Gigi's cheeks got hot.

He was laughing at her!

Gigi remembered the present.

"This is for you, Ojiisan," she said.

"Arigatoo," he said.

Gigi knew that meant "thank you."
Ojiisan carefully put the envelope
in his jacket pocket.

All the way home,

Mom and Ojiisan spoke in Japanese.

"Ojiisan says he got lost at the airport!

He couldn't read the signs,

and a nice woman helped him."

15

"Oh no!" thought Gigi.

"Ojiisan can't play tag,

and he can't read books with me."

This was not going well at all!

"At least we can play with Roscoe

and teach him tricks . . ."

Back at home, Roscoe was excited
to see everyone. Uh-oh . . .
"Roscoe!" Mom scolded.
Ojiisan said something in Japanese.
"What did he say?" Dad asked.
"He said, 'This is why dogs should
not live indoors,'" Mom said.
Dad showed Ojiisan to his room.

"Does Ojiisan hate Roscoe?"

Gigi asked her mom.

"No, hon.

Ojiisan just needs to get to know him better."

"I wanted to play tag and read books
with Ojiisan.
I wanted us to play with Roscoe
and teach him new tricks.
But we won't be able to do any of that,"
said Gigi.

19

Gigi began to cry.

"I don't think Ojiisan even likes me."

She began to cry even harder.

"Ojiisan loves you," Mom said.

"But why didn't he hug me
at the airport?" asked Gigi.

"Japanese people rarely hug.

We bow.

It took me a while to get used to it too!"
Mom said.

"Ojiisan laughed at me when I tried
to say konnichiwa," said Gigi.
"He wasn't laughing at you.
Sometimes he just laughs
when he doesn't know what to say,"
Mom said.

"But he didn't even open my present when I gave it to him!" Gigi said. "Most Japanese people his age think it's rude to open a present in front of the person who gave it to them," Mom explained.

There was so much about Japan

that Gigi didn't know!

"I can't even speak Japanese right!" she said.

"You've been doing great
with your words!" Mom said.

"Maybe Ojiisan can teach me words too?"
Gigi said hopefully.

"He would love that," said Mom.

"C'mon. Let's go see how he's doing."

Ojiisan said something
and pointed to the drawing
when they entered his room.
"What?" said Gigi.
It sounded like a Japanese word.
"He said, 'Thank you,'" Mom said.

26

Ojiisan laughed.

"My English is not so good," he said slowly.

"You teach me, OK?" he asked Gigi.

"Hai!" Gigi said.

Then Ojiisan gave Gigi a big package.

"Arigatoo!" she said.

Gigi began unwrapping it.

She remembered what her mom said
and stopped.

"Go ahead and open it!" Mom said.

Inside was the most perfect gift!

"Thank you, Ojiisan!" shouted Gigi.

Without thinking, she gave him a big hug.

"Oh!" he said, surprised.

Then he gave her a big hug back.

"You call me 'Ojiji,' OK?" Ojiisan said.

"That means grandpa," said Mom.

"We're going to have so much fun
together, Ojiji!" said Gigi.
Even Roscoe agreed.

GLOSSARY

Arigatoo **Thank you**

Hai Yes

Konnichiwa Hello or good afternoon

ROSCOE

Ojiisan A grandfather

Ojiji A nickname version of "grandfather." You would only say this to your own grandfather and only if you are close to him. It's like saying "grandpa."